T0380940

PROJECT EXTINCTION

Coloring & Spirograph Book

By Kimbra Eberly and Carissa Pignatelli

To order additional copies of this book, contact:
Xlibris
844-714-8691
www.Xlibris.com
Orders@Xlibris.com

Original Cover Art - Copyright©2024 Kimbra Eberly and Carissa Pignatelli
http://www.kimbraeberly.net

All original art - Copyright©2024 Kimbra Eberly and Carissa Pignatelli
http://projectextinction.com

Forward by Carissa Pignatelli

Editor - Margaret Chase
http://onwavestreet.com/margaret-chase

ISBN: Softcover   979-8-3694-2493-3 (sc)
         EBook   979-8-3694-2492-6 (e)

Print information available on the last page

Rev. date: 07/03/2024

Project Extinction

This Book Belongs To:

_____

Celebrating the beauty of animals and nature, perfect for animal lovers of all ages.

Image Index

1. Eberly, Kimbra North Atlantic Right Whale 2024, acrylic on canvas, Private Collection
2. Eberly, Kimbra North Atlantic Right Whale 2024, black line drawing, PC
3. Eberly, Kimbra Emperor Penguin 2024, acrylic on canvas, PC
4. Eberly, Kimbra Emperor Penguin 2024, black line drawing, PC
5. Eberly, Kimbra Araripe Manakin 2024, acrylic on canvas, PC
6. Eberly, Kimbra Araripe Manakin 2024, black line drawing, PC
7. Eberly, Kimbra - Pignatelli, Carissa Polar Bear 2024, acrylic on canvas, spirograph, PC
8. Eberly, Kimbra Polar Bear 2024, black line drawing, PC
9. Eberly, Kimbra - Pignatelli, Carissa Panda Bear 2024, acrylic on canvas, spirograph, PC
10. Eberly, Kimbra Panda Bear 2024, black line drawing, PC
11. Eberly, Kimbra Sunda Tiger 2024, acrylic on canvas, PC
12. Eberly, Kimbra Sunda Tiger 2024, black line drawing, PC
13. Eberly, Kimbra Grizzly Bears in Field 2024, acrylic on canvas, PC
14. Eberly, Kimbra Grizzly Bears in Field 2024, black line drawing, PC
15. Eberly, Kimbra - Pignatelli, Carissa African Lion 2024, acrylic on canvas, spirograph, PC
16. Eberly, Kimbra African Lion 2024, black line drawing, PC
17. Eberly, Kimbra - Pignatelli, Carissa Albino Alligator 2024, acrylic on canvas, spirograph, PC
18. Eberly, Kimbra Albino Alligator 2024, black line drawing, PC
19. Eberly, Kimbra White Rhino 2024, acrylic on canvas, PC
20. Eberly, Kimbra White Rhino 2024, black line drawing, PC
21. Pignatelli, Carissa Giraffe 2024, acrylic florescent paint on canvas, spirograph, PC
22. Eberly, Kimbra Giraffe 2024, black line drawing, PC
23. Eberly, Kimbra - Pignatelli, Carissa Elephant 2024, acrylic on canvas, spirograph, PC
24. Eberly, Kimbra Elephant 2024, black line drawing, PC
25. Eberly, Kimbra Vaquita Porpoise 2024, acrylic on canvas, PC
26. Eberly, Kimbra Vaquita Porpoise 2024, black line drawing, PC
27. Eberly, Kimbra - Pignatelli, Carissa Seahorse 2024, acrylic on canvas, spirograph, PC
28. Eberly, Kimbra Seahorse 2024, black line drawing, PC
29. Eberly, Kimbra - Pignatelli, Carissa Octopus 2024, acrylic on canvas, spirograph, PC
30. Eberly, Kimbra Octopus 2024, black line drawing, PC
31. Eberly, Kimbra Galapagos Penguin 2024, acrylic on canvas, PC
32. Eberly, Kimbra Galapagos Penguin 2024, black line drawing, PC

33. Eberly, Kimbra - Pignatelli, Carissa Hawksbill Turtle 2024, acrylic on canvas, spirograph, PC
34. Eberly, Kimbra Hawksbill Turtle 2024, black line drawing, PC
35. Eberly, Kimbra Monarch Butterfly 2024, acrylic on canvas, PC
36. Eberly, Kimbra Monarch Butterfly 2024, black line drawing, PC
37. Eberly, Kimbra Bumblebees 2024, acrylic on canvas, PC
38. Eberly, Kimbra Bumblebees 2024, black line drawing, PC

Contents

Acknowledgements.. vii

Charting a Course viii

SAVING THE OCEANS - SAVING THE ANIMALS.. 1

North Atlantic Right Whale.. 2

Penguin 4

Araripe Manakin 6

Polar Bear 8

Panda Bear 10

Sunda Tiger... 12

Grizzly Bear 14

African Lion 16

Albino Alligator.. 18

Rhinoceros 20

Giraffe 22

Elephant... 24

Vaquita Porpoise 26

Seahorse 28

Octopus.. 30

Galapagos Penguin 32

Hawksbill Turtle 34

Monarch Butterfly.. 36

North American Bumblebee.. 38

Acknowledgements

Kimbra Eberly

I am extremely grateful for the support I have received from many folks.

Margaret Chase, my editor, you have been invaluable, nurturing me along the way and affirming the need for this project. Working with you is easy and I value your friendship. You are one smart cookie.

Carissa, this project has been an amazing journey. We laughed, we cried, and we became closer friends. You are an amazing person.

Craig Spector, you have made an enormous difference in my life as a friend and mentor. You never stopped believing in me. I look forward to working on a project with you in the future.

To my family, for always being there for me. I love you all.

To all the artists that have helped and inspired me along the way, growing as a painter. Thank you.

Kenny, I am deeply grateful for your partnership as we continue to grow and strengthen together, passing 20 years. Wow! You are my rock.

Carissa Pignatelli

Kimbra, I've always had a deep love for diverse art forms and animals. Until now, I have never had the opportunity to bring them together. I'm grateful for your push during the times I needed it. Thank you for working with me to bring art and light into my life.

Brittany, you always encourage me to live life as creatively as possible. I'm happy to create something enjoyable for you and your children.

To my friends who love nature, I hope this honors our hiking adventures and conservation trips. Even though we may feel small in this world, there are so many things we can do as a collective to make the world a better place.

Charting a Course

Thank you for welcoming our artwork into your home. Your support benefits us as artists, and helps protect many endangered animals.

Kimbra and I, both animal enthusiasts, founded Project Extinction to showcase the beauty of endangered animals and to make learning about them enjoyable.

The alarming rate of species extinction is not only a concern for environmentalists; it is a wakeup call for humanity as a whole. When a species goes extinct, it weakens the intricate web of life that sustains us all.

This book showcases our favorite animals, and provides essential information about their existence. Your coloring and creative spirographs bring the images to life.

The spirograph is a geometric drawing toy and something I loved doing as a child. I still do. Did you know that diverse artists such as Salvador Dali, Picasso and Mondrian all produced art by using the spirograph? This timeless toy is so inspiring to me - we believe it will be for you too! One of the packages contains a spirograph kit.

Through the Project Extinction exhibit and coloring book, our goal is to motivate everyone to support organizations like the World Wildlife Fund for a sustainable future. For details on how you can help, see our references at the end of the book. Just by purchasing a coloring book, you are helping! We are so grateful to you for choosing us. This book contains only a handful of the thousands of animals that need your support. We hope you'll pour your love, imagination, and creativity into this book and develop a deep affection for these incredible creatures, just as we did.

Amidst our current global predicament, hope also shines brightly - a collective realization that we possess the power to effect meaningful change.

Carissa Pignatelli and Kimbra Eberly
June, 2024

SAVING THE OCEANS - SAVING THE ANIMALS

The ocean is one of our greatest sources of life on Earth. It provides us with more than half of the world's oxygen and is home to millions of species of marine life. The ocean also plays an enormous role in regulating our planet's climate, water cycle and more.

Plankton are the base of the marine food web. Without plankton we would have no fish and no food for millions of people. Without ocean life, many animals and people would starve. The temperatures of both the earth and its bodies of water are steadily warming. Warmer temperatures restrict the circulation of deep-sea nutrients that feed the plankton, interfering with their ability to multiply and disrupting the food chain.

Plants and animals help balance levels of greenhouse gases that heat the Earth. The migration of marine animals transfers nutrients all around the planet. Overall, ocean wildlife purifies, regulates and enhances the nutrient transfer system.

Clouds play a key role in making the Earth habitable. Without clouds forming over the ocean, rain would be rare, and the planet would become a desert. Our lakes and water supplies would dwindle a little more every year until nothing was left.

Clouds also regulate the amount of solar energy that reaches the surface and the amount of the Earth's energy that is radiated back into space. The more energy that is trapped by the planet, the warmer our climate will grow, as temperatures climb.

What kind of ocean will future generations have? The challenges are numerous: pollution, rising seas, ocean warming, oxygen depletion, and acidification. We can act now to put solutions into place.

The National Ocean Policy established by former President Barack Obama provides U.S. regions with support to develop "regional ocean plans" that empower local ocean stakeholders to represent their interests in decision making. Other countries, including China, Australia, the Philippines and various European nations have implemented similar practices.

Although scientists confirm that fish populations are declining, it is not too late for fish, sea turtles, dolphins, whales, and sharks to rebound in our lifetime. This will take coordinated and sustained action to correct environmental damage, and help oceans and marine life become healthy again. Together, we can make it happen.

The North Atlantic Right Whale is easily identified by the white calluses on its head, which are very noticeable against the whale's dark gray body. It has a broad back without a dorsal fin and a long arching mouth that begins above the eye. A baleen whale, it feeds by swimming through a swarm of plankton with its mouth open and its head slightly above the surface. Right whales are found more often in coastal waters, especially during the breeding season. Adult right whales are generally between 45 and 52 feet in length and can weigh up to 70 tons.

This whale is one of the most endangered of all large whales with a long history of human exploitation and no signs of recovery despite protection from whaling since the 1930s. It is now mostly found along the Atlantic coast of North America, where it is threatened by entanglement in fishing gear and ship collisions.

Status: Endangered
Population: 366 individuals, 70 females

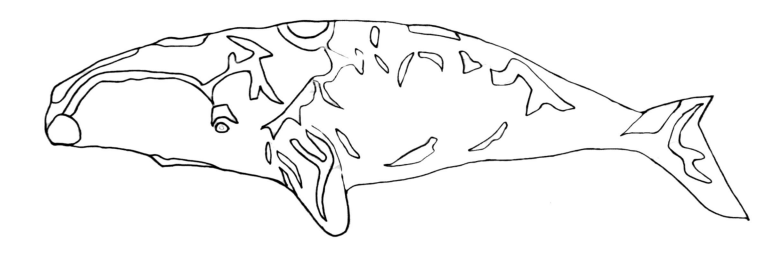

The Penguin is comprised of 18 species existing today. One of the most threatened and iconic is the Emperor Penguin, which is the largest, standing up to 3.5 feet tall. They are true Antarctic residents and are known to mate for life. The female lays her egg which is incubated for two months by the male while the female feeds at sea on creatures like squid and small fish. Parents take turns caring for their chicks.

The biggest threat right now is climate change. Emperor Penguins live and breed on the frozen ice. Warmer temperatures can affect chick hatching time, and therefore chicks may be born when food is more scarce.

Status: Endangered
Populations: Have declined by 50% in some places, and one colony off the Antarctic Peninsula has disappeared.

The Araripe Manakin, nicknamed "little soldier of Araripe," is considered one of the rarest birds in Brazil and the world. The male is black and white with a prominent, bright red helmetlike crown. In contrast, the females are mainly olive green. Their habitat is threatened due to agriculture and housing developments. They have an estimated 7,000 acres of forest left to survive in.

Status: Critically Endangered
Population: 1,000

The Polar Bear symbolizes the Arctic's endurance and power. Polar bears are the largest bear species and also the apex predators of the region.

Considered talented swimmers, polar bears can sustain a pace of six miles per hour by paddling with their front paws and holding their hind legs flat like a rudder. They have a thick layer of body fat and a water-repellent coat that insulates them from the cold air and water.

A polar bear dedicates more than half of its time hunting for food. Depending on the season, a polar bear may catch just one or two seals of every ten it hunts. To ensure survival, they rely on a diet of ringed and bearded seals, which are rich in fat.

Sea ice is crucial for polar bears as it enables them to travel, hunt, rest, mate, and even provides maternal dens in certain regions. Because of climate change, there has been a continuous loss of their sea ice habitat.

Status: Endangered
Population: 22,000-31,000

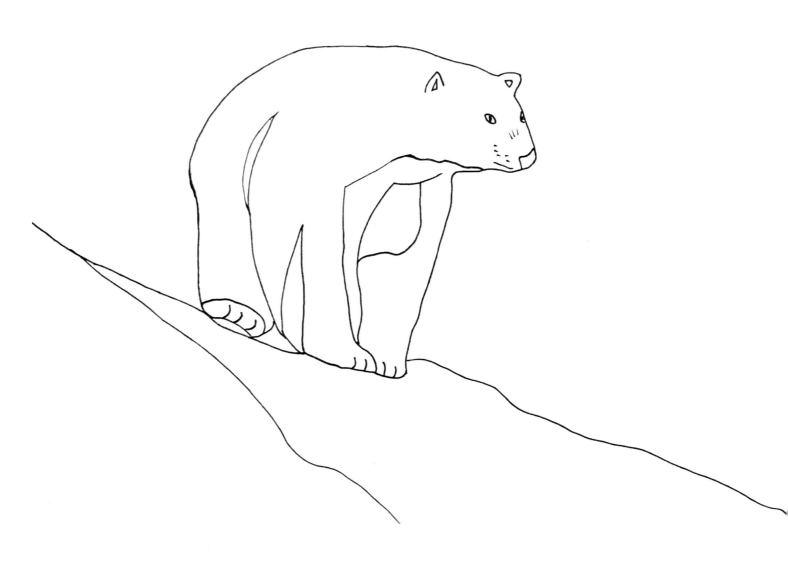

The Panda Bear lives mainly in temperate forests high in the mountains of southwest China, and subsists almost entirely on bamboo. They must eat 26 to 84 lbs. daily. They use their enlarged wrist bones that function as opposable thumbs.

A newborn panda is about the size of a stick of butter—about 1/900th the size of its mother—but females can grow up to about 200 lbs., while males can grow up to 300 lbs. These bears are excellent tree climbers despite their bulk.

Infrastructure such as dams, roads, and railways are causing habitat loss, preventing pandas from finding new bamboo forests and potential mates.

Status: Vulnerable
Population: 1,864

The Sunda Tiger is distinguished by heavy black stripes on its orange coat. The last of the Sunda Island tigers survive in the remaining patches of forest on the island of Sumatra. Accelerating deforestation and rampant poaching mean this noble creature could become extinct like its Javan and Balinese counterparts.

The habitat of the Sunda Tiger has been greatly reduced by deforestation from agriculture, specifically the palm oil plantations. On many parts of the island, timber harvesting is out of control to make way for palm oil farms. Illegal hunting for commercial gain is responsible for almost 80% of tiger deaths.

Status: Critically Endangered
Population: Less than 400

The Grizzly Bear is an iconic North American mammal, found in Alaska, parts of Canada, and portions of the northwestern United States. As humans take and use lands where grizzly bears live, the bears are forced to retreat to increasingly smaller untouched areas. Global warming appears to be exacerbating human-caused grizzly bear mortalities. Climate change is altering grizzly bears' habitats, making their environment less habitable due to rising temperatures, melting ice, and seasonal changes.

Status: Threatened

Population: There are currently about 55,000 wild grizzly bears located throughout North America, 30,000 of which are found in Alaska. Only 1,500 grizzlies remain in the lower 48 United States. Of these, around 800 are found in Montana.

The African Lion is a symbol of power, strength and courage. A lion's roar can be heard from five miles away. Lions are the supreme predators of the African savannah. These great hunters play a pivotal role in sustaining healthy ecosystems by maintaining balanced numbers of herbivores, such as zebras and wildebeests.

Habitats have shrunk as a result of human land use and climate change. Their current range is now just 8% of what it used to be. A recent study led by Panthera.org suggests that the targeted poaching of lions for their skin, teeth, claws, and bones accounts for 35% of known human-related lion killings.

Status: Vulnerable
Population: 20,000

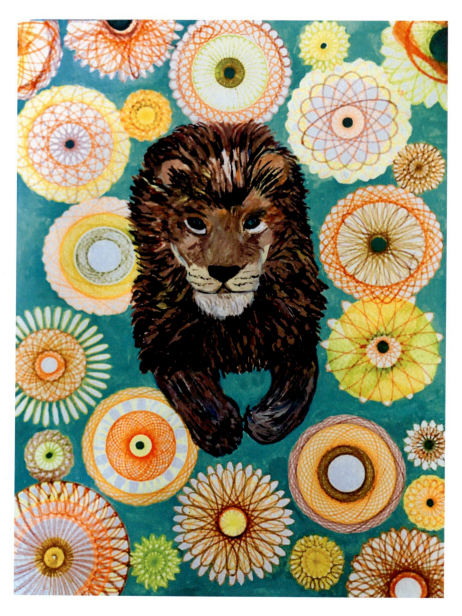

The Albino Alligator is exceptionally rare. Its unique appearance includes striking white skin and ruby-red eyes resulting from their albinism. This lack of pigment, though viewed as beautiful, has its downside. Most albino alligators rarely make it to adulthood because they are not able to camouflage themselves, making them easy targets in the wild. Their skin is extremely sensitive to sunlight and sunburn. Sanctuaries help these 'gators to live out a lifespan of fifty years or more.

Status: Critically Endangered
Population: 100-200

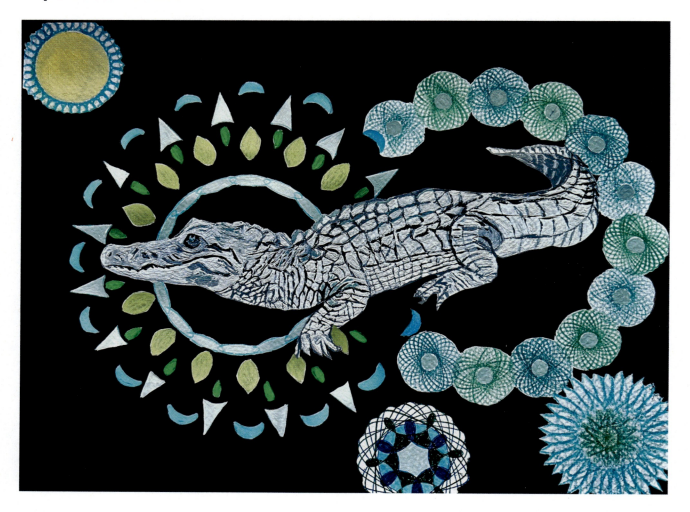

The Rhinoceros is the second-largest land mammal. Southern white rhinos were thought to be extinct in the late 19th century, but in 1895 a small population of fewer than 100 of these animals was discovered in Kwazulu-Natal, South Africa.

Two genetically different subspecies are the Northern and Southern white rhino, and are found in two different regions in Africa. As of today, there are only two of the Northern white rhino left, both female. These rare survivors live in the Ol Pejeta Conservancy in Kenya, and are protected round-the-clock by armed guards. Their near-extinction is due to decades of poaching for rhino horn.

Status: Endangered
Population: 27,000

The Giraffe is the world's tallest living land animal and can grow to be 18 feet tall. They eat only plants and use their long necks to reach leaves high up. Their tongues can grow up to 20 inches. The number of giraffes has plummeted approximately 40% over the past three decades. Some people refer to this as a 'silent extinction' because the decline has been so slow and gradual. The factors disrupting giraffes' way of life include habitat loss, poaching, drought, human-wildlife conflict, and civil unrest.

Status/Population: Current Red List of the eight assessed giraffe subspecies:
Nubian giraffe - critically endangered - 455 left
Rothschild's giraffe - near threatened - 1,399 left
Thornicroft's giraffe - vulnerable - 420 left
West African giraffe - vulnerable - 425 left

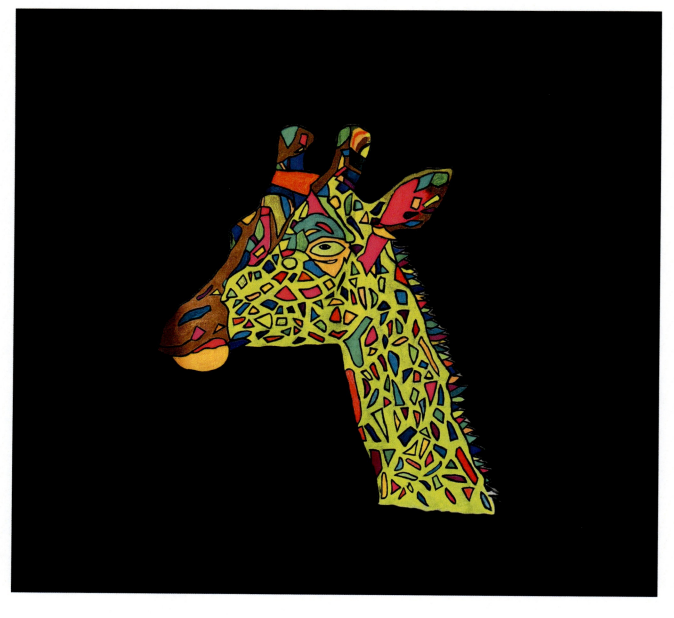

The Elephant was once common throughout Africa and Asia. However, over the last century, elephant populations have declined significantly. The greatest threat to African elephants is poaching for the illegal ivory trade, while Asian elephant populations are most at risk from habitat loss and resulting human-elephant conflict.

African elephants grow tusks and each individual can either be left-or right-tusked, and the one they use more is usually smaller because of wear and tear. Elephant tusks serve many purposes. These extended teeth can be used to protect the elephant's trunk, lift and move objects, gather food, and strip bark from trees. They can also be used for defense. During times of drought, elephants even use their tusks to dig holes to find water underground.

Status: Endangered
Population: 40,000

The Vaquita Porpoise wasn't discovered until 1958. A little over half a century later, we are on the brink of losing them forever. Vaquita are often inadvertently caught and drowned in gillnets used by illegal fishing operations in marine-protected areas within Mexico's Gulf of California. Gillnet bycatch negatively affects marine animals, sea turtles, sharks, sea birds, and endangered species. The population has dropped steeply in the last few years.

Status: Critically Endangered
Population: 10

The Seahorse has existed for thirteen million years, but unless action is taken it could become a creature of the past. Like most other species, both terrestrial and marine, seahorses, pipefishes, and sticklebacks face many threats. These include habitat loss, pollution, climate change, invasive species, and direct exploitation in the form of overfishing and bycatch. The extent of these threats varies from species to species.

Status: Threatened
Population: Twelve of the forty-two seahorse species have been listed as Vulnerable, and two listed as Endangered.

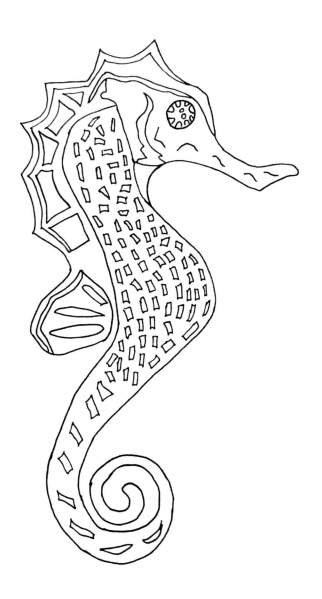

The Octopus possesses a striking anatomy. Its eight arms are the most obvious trait, and beneath the mottled skin there's an array of brains, one for each tentacle. They have three hearts, and each has an important function, so they're not just spares. Surprisingly, their life span is only two years.

The greatest threat to this creature is overfishing, which causes them to be caught and tangled in commercial fishing pots intended for other fish. Octopus, particularly the Umbrella Octopus, are the most endangered.

Status: Endangered
Population: Varies with each sub-species.

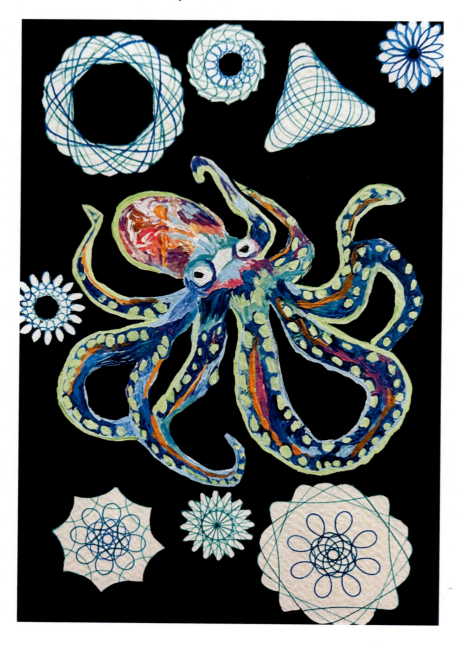

The Galapagos Penguin, one of the smallest of penguins, is found north of the equator in the Galapagos Islands. It typically measures 19 inches long, and weighs 5 lbs.

The Galapagos Penguin is threatened by pollution, bycatch and climate change. Non-native animal species introduced by humans such as dogs and cats carry diseases that can spread to penguins, and pose a threat as predators.

Status: Endangered
Population: Less than 2,000

The Hawksbill Turtle is found throughout the world's tropical oceans, in coral reefs. They feed mainly on sponges, and also eat sea anemones and jellyfish. Sea turtles are the living representatives and descendants of reptiles that have traveled the Earth's seas for the past one hundred million years. These turtles are a fundamental link in marine ecosystems and help maintain the health of coral reefs and sea grass beds.

Like other marine turtles, Hawksbills are threatened by the loss of nesting and feeding habitats, excessive egg collection, fishery-related mortality, pollution and coastal development. They are sought after for their beautiful brown and yellow shells.

Status: Endangered
Population: 8,000

The Monarch Butterfly embarks on a marvelous migratory phenomenon. They travel from 1,200 to more than 2,800 miles from the northeast United States and southeast Canada to the mountain forests in central Mexico, where they find the only perfect climate conditions to hibernate from the beginning of November to mid-March.

Milkweed is the sole plant on which monarchs lay their eggs, and the only source of food for the baby caterpillars. Urban planning and agricultural expansion have eliminated millions of acres of milkweed, leaving the butterflies vulnerable.

Adult monarchs are also vital pollinators. Many of the plants humans and other wildlife depend on (think fruits, vegetables and herbs) require pollinators to reproduce. The decline in monarch populations also affects the health of other pollinator populations, all of which directly impacts human food systems.

Status: Endangered
Population: 233,394

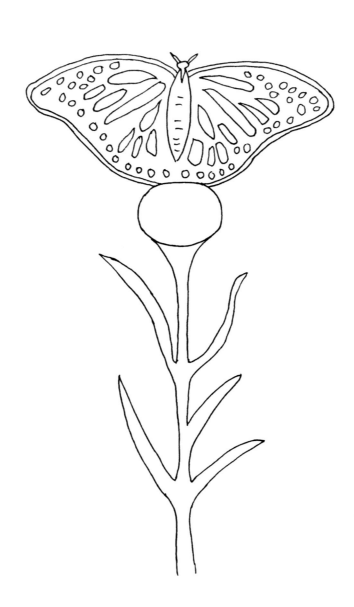

The North American Bumblebee is a species vulnerable to extinction because of habitat loss, pesticide use, disease and climate chaos. Of two hundred and fifty species worldwide, forty nine are located in North America and have been especially hard hit.

In the process of pollination insects move pollen from one plant to another, fertilizing the plants so that they can produce fruit, vegetables and seeds. If bees were to become extinct, the delicate balance of Earth's ecosystem would be profoundly disrupted and would affect global food supplies.

Status: Endangered
Population: The North American Bumblebee has disappeared or become very rare in sixteen states; the population have declined by nearly 90%.

REFERENCES

Together We Can Take Positive Action!

Conservation status used by the International Union for Conservation of Nature (IUCN):

Critically Endangered: highest risk of extinction in the wild

Endangered: higher risk of extinction in the wild

Vulnerable: high risk of extinction in the wild

Near-threatened: likely to become endangered in the near future

Bumblebees - https://environmentamerica.org/topics/save-the-bees/

Carolina Tiger Rescue - https://carolinatigerrescue.org

Center for Biological Diversity - https://www.biologicaldiversity.org/

Dolphins - https://www.dolphinsplus.com/blog/are-dolphins-endangered

Emperor Penguins - https://www.wwf.org.uk/learn/fascinating-facts/emperor-penguins

Galapagos Islands - https://www.worldwildlife.org/places/the-galapagos

Galapagos Penguin - https://abcbirds.org/bird/galapagos-penguin/

Greenpeace - https://www.greenpeace.org/usa/

Hawksbill Turtles - https://www.worldwildlife.org/species/hawksbill-turtle

International Fund for Animal Welfare - https://www.ifaw.org/

International Rhino Foundation - https://rhinos.org/about-rhinos/rhino-species/white-rhino/

Octopus Anatomy - https://now.northropgrumman.com/nine-brains-three-hearts-and-other-octopus-anatomy-facts#

Seahorses - https://seahorse.com

World Animal Protection - https://www.worldanimalprotection.us/

World Wildlife Fund - https://www.worldwildlife.org

Printed in the United States
by Baker & Taylor Publisher Services